Broadbea

Written by Matthew Lumb

Illustrated by Andrew Chellew

FIRST EDITION
Published in 2022 by
GREEN CAT BOOKS
19 St Christopher's Way
Pride Park
Derby
DE24 8JY

www.green-cat.shop

Cover art by Andrew Chellew.

Broadbean

Broadbean is a big bean. A massive bean. Some would say a huge bean. He has a broad body, broad arms and broad legs, and even broad fingers. When he was in his pod, none of the other beans had any space at all!

He is a rather heavy bean.
When he gets on the bus, the
whole thing leans to one side.

One day he tried to ride a bicycle, but there was not much left of it by the time he was done!

'You're too fat!' other beans would say to him. 'Go on a diet!' But what the other beans didn't realise is that Broadbean has tried many different diets. In fact, he would hardly eat anything bad or unhealthy.

He exercises too. He's always working out or running, but because of his size, it's not very easy for him!

Broadbean could not understand why he was this size. He always stood out in a crowd, which he didn't like. Sitting near him in the cinema, you wouldn't get to see much of the film!

One day, Broadbean decided to go to the park. But when he tried to sit on the swing, he soon found himself rubbing his bruised behind!

He played with his friend Beanie on the see-saw, but Broadbean ended up launching Beanie high into the air and landing in the nearby pond with a big splash!

'If I wanted to jump into the water, I would have visited the swimming pool!' spluttered Beanie, as he climbed out of the pond.

'I'm really sorry!' said Broadbean apologetically.

Broadbean decided that he must do something about his size. He decided to go and see the doctor.

As he sat in the waiting room, the other beans who had come to see the doctor had to move over to make space for him on the bench, but as it bowed under his weight, they soon found themselves crunched up beside him again.

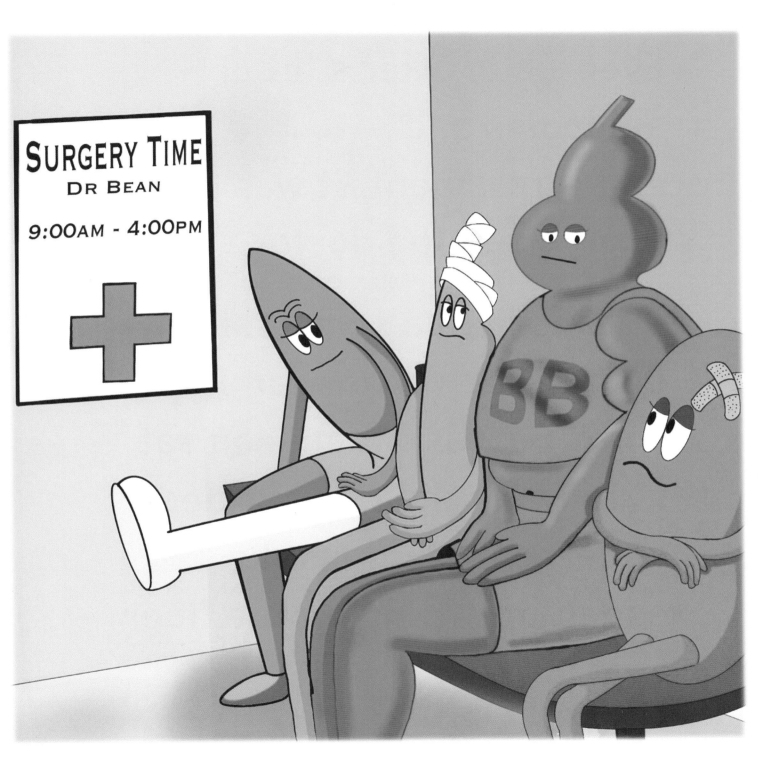

Eventually after a lot of apologies and embarrassment, it was his turn to see the doctor.

'Please take a seat,' said Doctor Bean. 'How can I help you?' But, as Broadbean sat in the tiny chair, it buckled underneath him and he ended up sitting on the floor again!

'I think I already see what the problem is,' laughed the doctor.

'I'm just too fat!' Broadbean wailed. 'Is there anything that can be done about it?'

'Perhaps we need to do some tests,' replied the doctor.

After a whole range of tests, the doctor rubbed his chin thoughtfully as he looked at the results.

'Well,' he started, 'We have checked your fat levels, your fitness levels, your food intake, but there is nothing wrong with you. I think that you are just going to have to accept the fact that you are just a very broad bean.'

Broadbean's face dropped.

'But, I think that there is something that you can do that will fit you perfectly.' the doctor continued. 'I have a friend who has a job that I believe would suit you right down to the ground.' Broadbean's face brightened. 'Really? What does he do?' 'Wrestling,' smiled Doctor Bean.

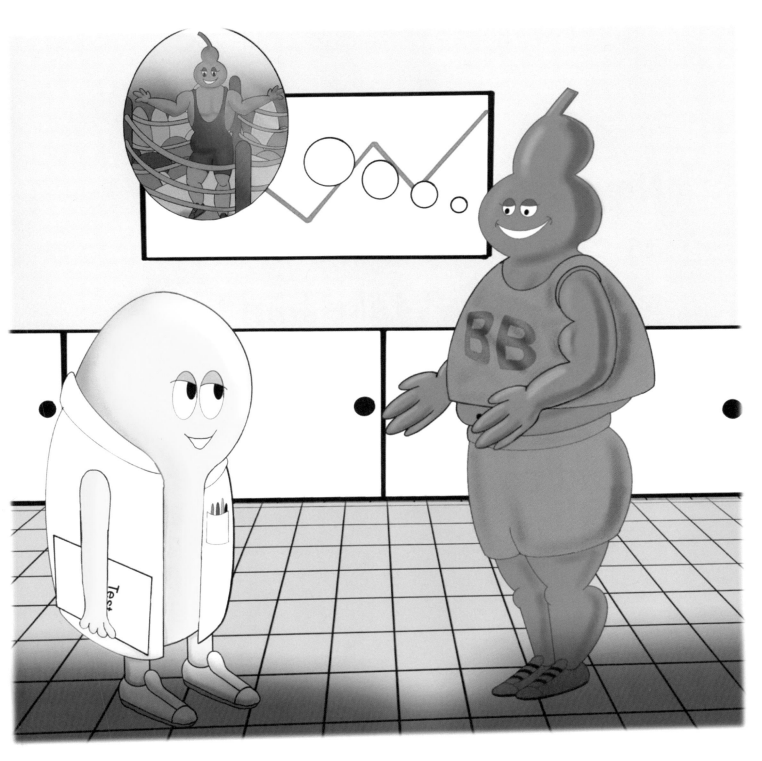

Now Broadbean is as happy as can be. Because of his size, it didn't take him long to become world champion, and people from far and wide would come to see him wrestle.

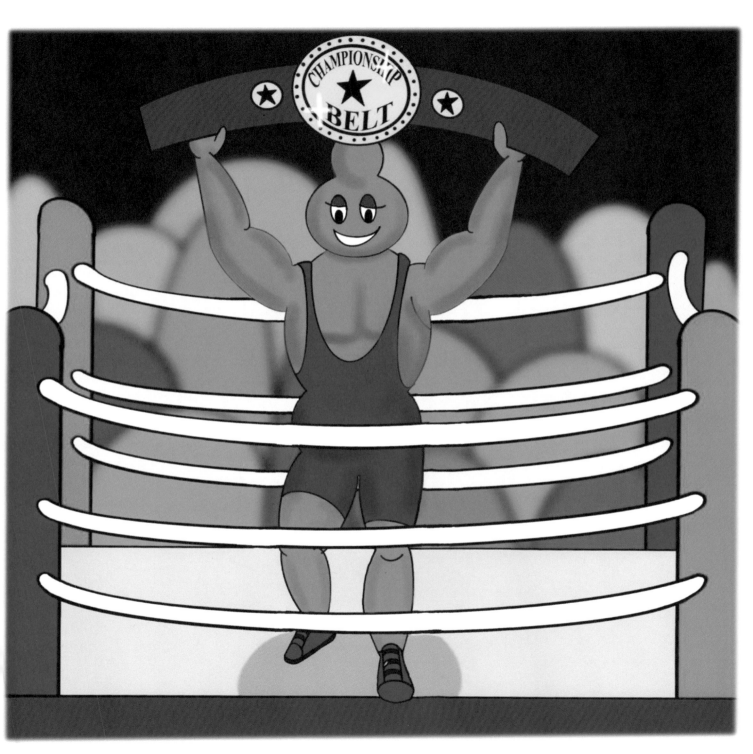

With his winnings, Broadbean thought that he would buy himself a new car. The problem was they were all so small...

...so he decided to get a monster truck instead!

So it just goes to show that sometimes, if you can't change what you are, then the best thing is to learn how to make the most of it!

If you would like more information about our books and authors,
or wish to submit a manuscript,
please visit www.green-cat.shop

Printed in Poland
by Amazon Fulfillment
Poland Sp. z o.o., Wrocław

88550780R00025